WINNIE-THE-POOH
AND FRIENDS

A. A. MILNE

Winnie-the-Pooh and Friends

Adapted by Stephen Krensky

With decorations by
ERNEST H. SHEPARD

Dutton Children's Books
New York

Pooh Goes Visiting
This presentation copyright © 2002 by the Trustees of the Pooh Properties
Pooh Invents a New Game
This presentation copyright © 2003 by the Trustees of the Pooh Properties
Tigger Comes to the Forest
This presentation copyright © 2002 by the Trustees of the Pooh Properties
This collection copyright © 2009 by the Trustees of the Pooh Properties

The publisher does not have any control over
and does not assume any responsibility for author or
third-party websites or their content.

CIP Data is available.
Published in the United States by Dutton Children's Books,
a division of Penguin Young Readers Group
345 Hudson Street, New York, New York 10014
www.penguin.com/youngreaders

Manufactured in China
First Edition

10 9 8 7 6 5 4 3 2 1

ISBN 978-0-525-42324-9

This edition created exclusively for Barnes & Noble Inc.,
under ISBN- 978-1-4351-2089-1

CONTENTS

POOH GOES
VISITING

A. A. MILNE

Pooh Goes Visiting

Adapted by Stephen Krensky

With decorations by
ERNEST H. SHEPARD

Dutton Children's Books
New York

1

POOH STEPS OUT

Winnie-the-Pooh was walking

through the forest one day,

humming proudly to himself.

He had made up a little hum

that very morning,

as he was doing his Stoutness Exercises.

"Tra-la-la, tra-la-la," he said,

stretching up as high as he could go.

And then *"Tra-la-la, tra-la—oh, help!—la,"*

as he tried to reach his toes.

He had said the hum over and over

until he had learned it by heart.

Now he was humming it

right through, properly.

Tra-la-la, tra-la-la,

Tra-la-la, tra-la-la,

Rum-tum-tiddle-um-tum.

Tiddle-iddle, tiddle-iddle,

Tiddle-iddle, tiddle-iddle,

Rum-tum-tum-tiddle-um.

Well, he was humming this hum,

when suddenly he came to a sandy bank.

And in the bank was a large hole.

"Aha!" said Pooh.

"If I know anything about anything,

that hole means Rabbit.

And Rabbit means Company.

And Company means Food."

So he bent down

and put his head into the hole.

"Is anybody at home?" he called out.

There was a scuffling noise

from inside the hole,

and then silence.

"What I said was,

'Is anybody at home?'"

called out Pooh very loudly.

"No!" said a voice.

"Bother!" said Pooh.

"Isn't there anybody here at all?"

"Nobody."

Pooh took his head out of the hole
and thought for a little.

"There must be somebody there,
because somebody must have *said*
'Nobody.'"

So he put his head back into the hole.

"Hallo, Rabbit, isn't that you?" he said.

"No," said Rabbit in a different sort of voice.

"But isn't that Rabbit's voice?" Pooh asked.

"I don't *think* so," said Rabbit.

"It isn't *meant* to be."

"Oh!" said Pooh.

He took his head out of the hole

and had another think.

Then he put it back in.

"Well," he said,

"could you very kindly

tell me where Rabbit is?"

"He has gone to see his friend

Pooh Bear," said Rabbit.

"But this *is* Me!" said Bear,

very much surprised.

"What sort of Me?" asked Rabbit.

"Pooh Bear."

"Are you sure?" said Rabbit.

"Quite, quite sure," said Pooh.

"Oh, well, then," said Rabbit,

"come in."

2

POOH HAS A LITTLE SOMETHING

So Pooh pushed and pushed and pushed his way through the hole, and at last he got in.

"You were quite right," said Rabbit, looking at him all over.

"It *is* you."

"Who did you think it was?" said Pooh.

"Well, I wasn't sure," said Rabbit.

"You know how it is in the forest.

One has to be *careful*.

What about a mouthful of something?"

Pooh always liked a little something

at eleven o'clock in the morning,

and he was very glad to see Rabbit

getting out the plates and mugs.

"Honey or condensed milk

with your bread?" asked Rabbit.

Pooh was so excited that he said, "Both."

And then, not wanting to seem greedy,

he added, "But don't bother

about the bread, please."

For a long time after that

he said nothing....

Until at last, humming to himself

in a rather sticky voice, he got up,

shook Rabbit lovingly by the paw,

and said that he must be going.

"Well, good-bye," said Rabbit.

"If you're sure you won't have

 any more."

"*Is* there any more?" asked Pooh quickly.

 Rabbit took the covers off the dishes.

"No, there isn't," he said.

"I thought not," said Pooh,

nodding to himself.

"Well, good-bye, then."

So Pooh started to climb

out of the hole.

He pulled with his front paws

and pushed with his back paws.

In a little while his nose

was out in the open again…

and then his ears…

and then his front paws…

and then his shoulders…

and then—

"Oh, help!" said Pooh.

"I'd better go back.

Oh, bother!" said Pooh.

"I shall have to go on.

I can't do either!" said Pooh.

"Oh, help *and* bother!"

3

POOH REMAINS IN A TIGHT PLACE

Now by this time

Rabbit wanted to go for a walk too.

Finding his front door full,

he went out the back,

and came round to Pooh.

"Hallo, are you stuck?"

he asked.

"N-no," said Pooh carelessly.

"Just resting and thinking

and humming to myself."

"Here, give us a paw," said Rabbit.

Pooh stretched out a paw,

and Rabbit pulled and

pulled and pulled....

"Ow!" cried Pooh. "You're hurting."

"The fact is," said Rabbit,

"you're stuck."

"It all comes," said Pooh crossly,

"of not having front doors

   big enough."

"It all comes," said Rabbit sternly,

"of eating too much.

   I thought at the time—

   only I didn't want

   to say anything—

   that one of us was eating

   too much.

   And I knew it wasn't *me*.

   Well, well, I shall go and fetch

   Christopher Robin."

Christopher Robin lived at the other

end of the forest.

When he came back with Rabbit,

he saw the front half of Pooh.

"Silly old Bear," he said,

in such a loving voice

that everybody felt

quite hopeful again.

"I was just beginning to think,"

said Pooh, sniffing slightly,

"that Rabbit might never be able

to use his front door again.

And I should *hate* that."

"So should I," said Rabbit.

"Use his front door again?"

said Christopher Robin.

"Of course he'll use

his front door again."

"Good," said Rabbit.

"If we can't pull you out, Pooh,"

said Christopher Robin,

"we might push you back."

Rabbit scratched

his whiskers thoughtfully.

He pointed out that,

once Pooh was pushed back,

he was back.

Of course, nobody was more glad

to see Pooh than *he* was.

Still, some lived in trees

and some lived underground, and—

"You mean I'd *never* get out?" said Pooh.

"I mean," said Rabbit,

"that having got *so* far,

it seems a pity to waste it."

Christopher Robin nodded.

"Then there's only one thing to be done,"

he said. "We shall have to wait

for you to get thin again."

"How long does getting thin take?"

asked Pooh anxiously.

"About a week, I should think,"

said Christopher Robin.

"But I can't stay here for a *week!*"

said Pooh.

"You can *stay* here all right,

silly old Bear,"

said Christopher Robin.

"It's getting you out which is

so difficult."

"We'll read to you," said Rabbit cheerfully.

"And I hope it won't snow.

And I say, as you're taking up

a good deal of room,

do you mind if I use your back legs as

a towel-horse?

"Because, I mean, there they are—

doing nothing—

and it would be very convenient."

"A week!" said Pooh gloomily.

"What about meals?"

"I'm afraid no meals,"

said Christopher Robin,

"because of getting thinner quicker."

Pooh began to sigh,

and then found he couldn't

because he was so tightly stuck.

A tear rolled down his eye.

"Then," he said,

"would you read a Sustaining Book

that would help and comfort

a Wedged Bear in Great Tightness?"

"Of course," said Christopher Robin.

4

POOH REGAINS
HIS FREEDOM

So for a week

Christopher Robin read

at the North end of Pooh.

And Rabbit hung his washing

on the South end.

And in between Pooh felt himself

getting slenderer and slenderer.

At the end of the week

Christopher Robin said, *"Now!"*

He took hold of Pooh's front paws,

and Rabbit took hold

of Christopher Robin.

And all of Rabbit's friends and

relations took hold of Rabbit.

Then they all pulled together....

For a long time Pooh only said

"Ow!"... and *"Oh!"*...

Then, all of a sudden, he said *"Pop!"*

just as if a cork

were coming out of a bottle.

And Christopher Robin and Rabbit

and all Rabbit's friends and relations

went head-over-heels backwards . . .

and on the top of them

came Winnie-the-Pooh—free!

So, with a nod of thanks to his friends,

Pooh went on with his walk

through the forest,

humming proudly to himself.

But Christopher Robin

looked after him lovingly,

and said to himself,

"Silly old Bear!"

POOH INVENTS
A NEW GAME

A. A. MILNE

Pooh Invents a New Game

Adapted by Stephen Krensky

With decorations by
ERNEST H. SHEPARD

Dutton Children's Books
New York

1

POOH HAS A MOVING EXPERIENCE

One day Winnie-the-Pooh

was walking through the Forest

toward a wooden bridge.

He was trying to make up

a piece of poetry about

fir-cones.

He picked up a fir-cone

and looked at it.

"This is a very good fir-cone,"

Pooh said to himself,

"and something ought

to rhyme with it."

But he couldn't think of anything.

And then this came into his head suddenly:

Here is a myst'ry

About a little fir-tree.

Owl says it's his tree,

And Kanga says it's her tree.

"Which doesn't make sense," said Pooh,

"because Kanga doesn't live in a tree."

He had just come to the bridge

and was not looking where

he was going.

Then he tripped over something,

and the fir-cone jerked out

of his paw into the river.

"Bother," said Pooh as it

floated under the bridge.

He looked at the river

as it slipped slowly away beneath him…

and suddenly, there was his fir-cone

slipping away too.

"That's funny," said Pooh.

"I dropped it on the other side,

and it came out on this side!

I wonder if it would do it again?"

And he went back for more fir-cones.

It did. It kept on doing it.

Then he dropped two in at once,

and leaned over the bridge

to see which of them

would come out first.

And one of them did.

But as they were both the same size,

Pooh didn't know if it was the one

that he wanted to win, or the other one.

So the next time he dropped in

one big one and one little one.

The big one came out first,

which was what he had said

it would do.

And the little one came out last,

which was what he had said

it would do.

So he had won twice.

And when he went home for tea,

he had won thirty-six and lost

twenty-eight, which meant

that he was—

well, you take twenty-eight from

thirty-six, and *that's* what he was.

Instead of the other way around.

2

EEYORE APPEARS UNEXPECTEDLY

That was the beginning

of the game called Poohsticks,

which Pooh invented.

He and his friends used to play it

on the edge of the Forest.

But they played with sticks

instead of fir-cones

because sticks were easier to mark.

Now one day Pooh and Piglet

and Rabbit and Roo

were all playing Poohsticks together.

They had dropped their sticks in

when Rabbit said "Go!"

Then they had hurried across

to the other side of the bridge,

and now they were all leaning

over the edge,

waiting to see whose stick

would come out first.

But it was a long time coming,

because the river was lazy that day,

and hardly seemed to mind

if it didn't ever get there at all.

"I can see mine!" cried Roo.

"No, I can't, it's something else.

Can you see yours, Piglet?

I thought I could see mine,

but I couldn't.

There it is!

No, it isn't.

Can you see yours, Pooh?"

"No," said Pooh.

"I expect my stick's stuck," said Roo.

"Rabbit, my stick's stuck.

Is your stick stuck, Piglet?"

"They always take longer

than you think," said Rabbit.

"How long do you *think* they'll take?"

asked Roo.

"I can see yours, Piglet,"

said Pooh suddenly.

"Mine's a sort of grayish one,"

said Piglet,

not daring to lean too far over

in case he fell in.

"Yes, that's what I can see.

It's coming over to my side."

Rabbit leaned over further than ever,

looking for his stick.

And Roo wriggled up and down,

calling out, "Come on, stick!

Stick, stick, stick!"

And Piglet got very excited

because his was the only one

which had been seen.

That meant he was winning.

"It's coming!" said Pooh.

"Are you *sure* it's mine?"

squeaked Piglet.

"Yes, because it's gray.

A big gray one.

Here it comes! A very—

big—gray—

Oh, no, it isn't, it's Eeyore."

And out floated Eeyore.

"Eeyore!" cried everybody.

Looking very calm,

very dignified,

with his legs in the air,

Eeyore came out from

beneath the bridge.

"It's Eeyore!" cried Roo,

terribly excited.

"Is that so?" said Eeyore,

getting caught up by a little eddy,

and turning around three times.

"I didn't know you were playing,"

said Roo.

"I'm not," said Eeyore.

"Eeyore, what *are* you doing there?"

said Rabbit.

"I'll give you three guesses, Rabbit.

Digging holes in the ground?

Wrong.

Leaping from branch to branch

of an oak-tree?

Wrong.

Waiting for somebody to help me

out of the river?

Right."

3

POOH GETS
AN IDEA

"But, Eeyore," said Pooh in distress,

"what can we—I mean, how shall

we—do you think if we———"

"Yes," said Eeyore.

"One of those would be

just the thing.

Thank you, Pooh."

"He's going *round* and *round*,"

said Roo, much impressed.

There was a moment's silence

while everybody thought.

"I've got a sort of idea,"

said Pooh at last.

"If we all threw stones and things into

the river on *one* side of Eeyore,

the stones would make waves,

and the waves would wash him

to the other side."

"That's a very good idea, Pooh,"

said Rabbit.

"Supposing we hit him by mistake?"

said Piglet anxiously.

"Or supposing you missed him

by mistake," said Eeyore.

But Pooh had got the biggest

stone he could carry,

and was leaning over the bridge,

holding it in his paws.

"I'm not throwing it,

I'm dropping it, Eeyore,"

he explained.

"And then I can't miss—

I mean I can't hit you.

Could you stop turning round

for a moment,

because it muddles me rather?"

"Now, Pooh," said Rabbit,

"when I say 'Now!'

you can drop it.

Piglet, give Pooh

a little more room.

Get back a bit there, Roo.

Are you ready?"

"No," said Eeyore.

"Now!" said Rabbit.

Pooh dropped his stone.

There was a loud splash,

and Eeyore disappeared....

It was an anxious moment

for the watchers

on the bridge.

They looked and looked....

And even the sight

of Piglet's stick

coming out a little in front of Rabbit's

didn't cheer them up as much

as you would have expected.

And then something gray

showed for a moment

by the river bank…

and it got slowly bigger and bigger…

and at last Eeyore was coming out.

With a shout

everyone rushed off the bridge,

pushing and pulling at Eeyore.

And soon he was standing among

them again on dry land.

"Well done, Pooh," said Rabbit kindly.

"That was a good idea of ours.

But how did you fall in, Eeyore?"

"I didn't," said Eeyore.

"I was BOUNCED."

"Oo," said Roo excitedly.

"Did somebody push you?"

"Somebody BOUNCED me.
I was just thinking by the side
of the river—when I received
a very loud BOUNCE."

"Oh, Eeyore!" said everybody.

"Who did it?" asked Roo.

Eeyore didn't answer.

"I expect it was Tigger,"

said Piglet nervously.

"But Eeyore," said Pooh,

"was it a Joke or an Accident?

I mean—"

"I didn't stop to ask, Pooh.

I just floated to the surface,

and said to myself, 'It's wet.'"

"And where was Tigger?"

asked Rabbit.

4

CHRISTOPHER ROBIN SETTLES THINGS

Before Eeyore could answer,

there was a loud noise behind them.

Then through the hedge

came Tigger himself.

"Hallo, everybody,"

said Tigger cheerfully.

"Hallo, Tigger," said Roo.

"Tigger," Rabbit said solemnly,

"what happened just now?"

"Just when?" said Tigger

a little uncomfortably.

"When you bounced Eeyore

into the river."

"I didn't bounce him."

"You bounced me,"

   said Eeyore gruffly.

"I didn't really.

   I had a cough,

   and I happened to be behind Eeyore.

   '*Grrrr—oppp—ptschschschz,*' I said."

"That's what I call bouncing,"

   said Eeyore.

"Very unpleasant habit.

   I don't mind Tigger being in the Forest.

   It's a large Forest,

   and there's plenty of room to

   bounce in it."

"But I don't see why he should come

into *my* little corner of it,

and bounce there."

"I didn't bounce, I coughed,"

said Tigger crossly.

"Bouncy or coffy," said Eeyore,

"it's all the same at the bottom

of the river."

"Well," said Rabbit,

"all I can say is—

well, here's Christopher Robin,

so *he* can say it."

Christopher Robin had come down

from the Forest to the bridge,

feeling all sunny and careless.

But when he saw all the animals there,

he knew it wasn't that kind of afternoon.

"It's like this," said Rabbit. "Tigger—"

"No, I didn't," said Tigger.

"Well, anyhow, there I was,"

said Eeyore.

"But I don't think he meant to,"

said Pooh.

"He just *is* bouncy," said Piglet,

"and he can't help it."

"Try bouncing *me,* Tigger,"

said Roo eagerly.

"Eeyore, Tigger's going to try *me.*"

"Yes, yes," said Rabbit,

"we don't all want to speak at once.

The point is, what does

Christopher Robin think?"

"All I did was cough," said Tigger.

"He bounced," said Eeyore.

"Well, I sort of boffed," said Tigger.

"Hush!" said Rabbit,

holding up his paw.

"What do you say, Christopher Robin?"

"Well," said Christopher Robin,

not quite sure what it was all about,

"*I* think—"

"Yes?" said everybody.

"*I* think we all ought to play

Poohsticks."

So they did.

And Eeyore,

who had never played it before,

won more times than anybody else.

TIGGER COMES
TO THE FOREST

99

A. A. MILNE

Tigger Comes
to the Forest

Adapted by Stephen Krensky

With decorations by
ERNEST H. SHEPARD

Dutton Children's Books
New York

101

1

TIGGER MAKES AN APPEARANCE

Winnie-the-Pooh woke up suddenly

in the night and listened.

Then he got out of bed and lit his candle.

He stumped across the room

to see if anyone was trying

to get into his honey-cupboard.

They weren't, so he stumped back again
and got into bed.

Then he heard the noise again.

"Is that you, Piglet?" he said.

But it wasn't.

"Come in, Christopher Robin."

But Christopher Robin didn't.

"Worraworraworraworraworra,"

said Whatever-it-was.

"What can it be?" thought Pooh.

"It isn't a growl,

and it isn't a purr,

and it isn't a bark.

It's a noise made by a strange animal.

And he's making it outside my door.

So I shall get up

and ask him not to do it."

Pooh got out of bed

and opened his front door.

"Hallo!" said Pooh.

"Hallo!" said Whatever-it-was.

"Who is it?" said Pooh.

"Me," said a voice.

"Oh!" said Pooh.

"Well, come here. I'm Pooh."

"I'm Tigger," said Tigger.

"Oh!" said Pooh.

"Does Christopher Robin

know about you?"

"Of course he does," said Tigger.

"Well," said Pooh,

"it's the middle of the night,

which is a good time

for going to sleep.

Tomorrow morning we'll have

some honey for breakfast.

Do Tiggers like honey?"

"They like everything," said Tigger.

"If they like going to sleep

on the floor," said Pooh,

"I'll go back to bed.

Good night."

When he awoke in the morning,

the first thing he saw was Tigger

looking at himself in the mirror.

"Hallo!" said Pooh.

"Hallo!" said Tigger.

"I've found somebody just like me."

Pooh got out of bed,

and began to explain

what a mirror was.

"Excuse me a moment," said Tigger.

"There's something climbing up your table."

With one loud

Worraworraworraworraworra

he jumped at the end of the tablecloth,

pulled it to the ground,

and wrapped himself up in it three times.

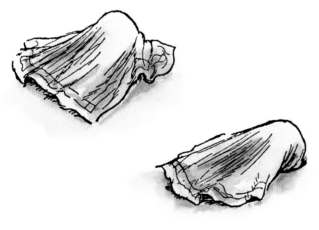

After a terrible struggle,

he got his head into the daylight again.

"Have I won?" he said cheerfully.

"That's my tablecloth," said Pooh,

as he began to unwind Tigger.

"I wondered what it was," said Tigger.

Pooh put the cloth back on the table.

Then he put a large honey-pot

on the cloth,

and they sat down to breakfast.

Tigger took a large mouthful of honey,

and then looked up at the ceiling.

He made exploring noises

and considering noises

and what-have-we-got-*here* noises.

Then he said in a very decided voice:

"Tiggers don't like honey."

"Oh!" said Pooh.

"I thought they liked everything."

"Everything except honey," said Tigger.

Pooh said that as soon as

he had finished,

he would take Tigger

to Piglet's house.

There Tigger could try

some of Piglet's haycorns.

"Thank you, Pooh," said Tigger.

"Haycorns is really

what Tiggers like best."

2

TIGGER MEETS
A VERY SMALL
ANIMAL

So after breakfast

Pooh and Tigger went round

to see Piglet.

Pooh explained as they went

that Piglet was a Very Small Animal

who didn't like bouncing.

So Pooh asked Tigger

not to be too Bouncy at first.

Tigger, who had been hiding

behind trees

and jumping out on Pooh's shadow,

said that Tiggers were only bouncy

before breakfast.

So by and by they knocked

at the door of Piglet's house.

"Hallo, Pooh," said Piglet.

"Hallo, Piglet. This is Tigger."

"Oh, is it?" said Piglet.

He edged round to the other side

of the table.

"I thought Tiggers

were smaller than that."

"Not the big ones," said Tigger.

"They like haycorns," said Pooh.

"And poor Tigger

hasn't had any breakfast."

Piglet pushed the bowl of haycorns

towards Tigger.

"Help yourself," he said.

Tigger filled his mouth with haycorns.

After a long munching noise, he said:

"Ee-ers o i a-ors."

"What?" said Pooh and Piglet.

"Skoos ee," said Tigger,

and went outside for a moment.

When he came back, he said firmly:

"Tiggers don't like haycorns."

"You said

　they liked everything

　except honey," said Pooh.

"Everything except honey

　and haycorns,"

　explained Tigger.

"Oh, I see!" said Pooh.

"What about thistles?" asked Piglet.

"Thistles," said Tigger,

"is what Tiggers like best."

"Then let's go along and see Eeyore,"

said Piglet.

So the three of them went.

3

TIGGER TRIES TO
EAT A THISTLE

After they had walked and walked,

they came to the part of the Forest

where Eeyore was.

"Hallo, Eeyore!" said Pooh.

"This is Tigger."

Eeyore walked all round Tigger one way.

Then he turned and walked

all round him the other way.

"What did you say it was?" he asked.

"Tigger."

"Ah!" said Eeyore.

"He's just come," explained Piglet.

"Ah!" said Eeyore again.

He thought for a long time and then said:

"When is he going?"

Pooh explained that Tigger

was a great friend of Christopher Robin's,

who had come to stay in the Forest.

"And Tiggers always eat thistles.

That was why we came to see you, Eeyore."

Eeyore led the way

to the most thistly-looking patch of thistles

that ever was.

"A little patch I was keeping

for my birthday," he said.

"But, after all, what are birthdays?

Here today and gone tomorrow.

Help yourself, Tigger."

Tigger thanked him

and looked a little anxiously at Pooh.

"Are these really thistles?" he whispered.

"Yes," said Pooh.

"What Tiggers like best?"

"That's right," said Pooh.

"I see," said Tigger.

So he took a large mouthful,

and he gave a large crunch.

"Ow!" he said.

He sat down and put his paw

in his mouth.

"What's the matter?" asked Pooh.

"Hot!" mumbled Tigger,

shaking his head

to get the prickles out.

"Tiggers don't like thistles."

"But you said," began Pooh,

"that Tiggers like everything

except honey and haycorns."

"*And* thistles," said Tigger.

Pooh looked at him sadly.

"What are we going to do?"

he asked Piglet.

Piglet knew the answer to that.

They must go and see

Christopher Robin.

"You'll find him with Kanga,"

said Eeyore.

Pooh nodded and called to Tigger.

"We'll go and see Kanga.

She's sure to have

lots of breakfast for you."

"Come on!" Tigger said,

and he rushed off.

4

IN WHICH

TIGGER FINALLY
EATS BREAKFAST

Pooh and Piglet walked slowly after Tigger.

And as they walked

Piglet said nothing,

because he couldn't think of anything.

And Pooh said nothing,

because he was thinking of a poem.

And when he had thought of it,

he began:

What shall we do about

poor little Tigger?

If he never eats nothing, he'll

never get bigger.

He doesn't like honey and haycorns

and thistles

Because of the taste and because of

the bristles.

And all the good things which an

animal likes

Have the wrong sort of swallow or

too many spikes.

Tigger had been bouncing

in front of them all this time,

turning round every now and then

to ask, "Is this the way?"

Now at last they came to

Kanga's house,

and there was Christopher Robin.

Tigger rushed up to him.

"Oh, there you are, Tigger!"

said Christopher Robin.

"I knew you'd be somewhere."

"I've been finding things in the Forest,"

said Tigger importantly.

"I've found a pooh and a piglet

and an eeyore.

But I can't find any breakfast."

Pooh and Piglet explained

what had been happening.

"Don't *you* know what Tiggers like?"

asked Pooh.

"I expect if I thought very hard I should,"

said Christopher Robin.

"But I *thought* Tigger knew."

"I do," said Tigger.

"Everything there is in the world

except honey and haycorns and—

what were those hot things called?"

"Thistles."

"Yes, and those."

"Oh, well then," said Christopher Robin,

"Kanga can give you some breakfast."

So they went into Kanga's house.

And Roo said, "Hallo, Pooh,"

and "Hallo, Piglet" once,

and "Hallo, Tigger" twice,

because he had never said it before

and it sounded funny.

Then they told Kanga what they wanted.

"Well, look in my cupboard, Tigger dear,"

Kanga said very kindly,

"and see what you'd like."

But the more Tigger put his nose

into this and his paw into that,

the more things he found

which Tiggers didn't like.

"What happens now?" he said

when he had tried everything

in the cupboard.

Kanga, Christopher Robin, and Piglet

were all standing round Roo,

watching him have his Extract of Malt.

"Must I?" said Roo.

"Now, Roo dear," said Kanga,

"you remember what you promised."

"What is it?" whispered Tigger to Piglet.

"His Strengthening Medicine," said Piglet.

"He hates it."

So Tigger came closer, and he leaned over

the back of Roo's chair.

Suddenly he put out his tongue,

and took one large golollop.

"Oh!" said Kanga,

pulling the spoon out of Tigger's mouth.

But the Extract of Malt was gone.

"Tigger *dear!*" said Kanga.

"He's taken my medicine,"

  sang Roo happily.

"He's taken my medicine!

  He's taken my medicine!"

  Then Tigger looked up at the ceiling.

  He closed his eyes,

  and his tongue went round and round.

  A peaceful smile came over his face.

"So *that's* what Tiggers like!" he said.

Which explains why he always lived

at Kanga's house afterwards.

Tigger had Extract of Malt

for breakfast, dinner, and tea.

And sometimes, when Kanga thought

Tigger wanted strengthening,

he had a spoonful or two

of Roo's breakfast as medicine.

"But *I* think," said Piglet to Pooh,

"that he's been strengthened

quite enough."